Wilhelmina's Butterflies

By: Clarice Thornton Davis
Illustrated By: Dwight Nacaytuna

To order additional copies of this book, contact:
Xlibris LLC
1-888-795-4274
www.Xlibris.com
Orders@Xlibris.com

DEDICATION

For my family, friends,
and readers everywhere.

Wilhelmina's lips moved softly. "Franz Schubert's music is so beautiful" and she began humming along to Ave Maria. "OUCH!" she yelled, waking up holding a large pillow. She felt so silly, and immediately realized it was Leon's way of waking her up. Her big brother was a jokester, and he seemed to enjoy teasing her. He laughed as Wilhelmina stuck out her tongue, smoothed her hair, and jumped out of bed. "What's that awful noise?" asked Leon.

"It's not awful and it's not noise" Wilhelmina shouted, and walked over to the radio, listened to the music, and turned it up a notch. Before going to bed last night, Wilhelmina decided not to set her alarm as she usually did. "Tomorrow I want to awake to the music I love. I want to be awakened by an orchestra", she told herself. So, she tuned the radio to her favorite classical music station and set the alarm to wake her up at 7:00.

Wilhelmina turned and saw the jokester leave the room, shaking his head and rolling his eyes toward the ceiling. "Does anyone understand?" Wilhelmina whispered to herself. Her family, friends, and even her teachers all wondered why an eight year old was so interested in classical music. Whenever they asked her why she listened to it so much, her usual reply was "I like the sounds of the instruments and the music relaxes me. I imagine myself playing in the orchestra whenever I hear it".

Dressing quickly, Wilhelmina made sure her outfit was neat and her hair just right. She ran downstairs, gave her mom a good morning kiss and sat in front of a warm bowl of cereal. "Good morning, Wilhelmina", Mom smiled. You mean "great morning", Wilhelmina beamed. "I've waited for this day for a long time. I'm so excited". "Excited about what?" her brother questioned. Wilhelmina gave him a wide grin. "The entire third grade is going to Symphony Hall today", she announced. "That's wonderful, Wilhelmina" her mom said. Leon laughed and rolled his eyes toward the ceiling again.

Wilhelmina sat at the table and stared at the bowl of hot cereal. Her stomach suddenly felt strange. "Mom, I don't feel like eating". Wilhelmina's mom felt her daughter's head and smiled. "You're okay Wilhelmina. You probably have butterflies", she explained. That didn't make sense to Wilhelmina, but she managed to eat a little. She gave Mom a hug, scooped up her backpack and gave her bossy Pekingese, Tattoo, a pat on the head before rushing off to her bus stop.

As Wilhelmina hopped onto the school bus, she greeted Mr. Luigi, the driver, with a happy smile. "We're going to Symphony Hall today", she announced. Some of the children on the bus groaned as Wilhelmina found her seat. Mr. Luigi chuckled and said "I wish I could be as lucky". Wilhelmina found her seat beside her best friend, Penny. "Are you ready?" Penny asked with a bright grin. "I can hardly wait" said Wilhelmina. She grabbed her stomach and thought to herself, "butterflies?"

The door to the classroom was open and a smiling Miss Harris, Wilhelmina's teacher, was busy greeting each child. Wilhelmina liked the way Miss Harris said each person's name as they entered the classroom. "Good morning, Wilhelmina" she smiled. "Great morning" giggled Wilhelmina. Miss Harris looked at her with raised eyebrows. Then she remembered why Wilhelmina was in such a wonderful mood, and winked. The other students were busy turning in homework, reading, and chatting. Wilhelmina joined Penny at the bookshelf and they each chose a book to read for their next book event.

As Miss Harris closed the door, she asked for everyone's attention. "We'll go to music class first today, and from there we'll leave for the concert at Symphony Hall". Wilhelmina looked towards Penny and grabbed her stomach again. Penny frowned and Wilhelmina mouthed "I'm okay". To Wilhelmina, Penny was the only person who respected her love of classical music. She even listened to the music Wilhelmina played on her computer, and seemed to enjoy it. Grumbling began to grow from Wilhelmina's classmates as they formed a line to go to the music room.

Their teacher reminded them that this would be a great experience and to be happy that they were one of the classes chosen to attend the concert. On hearing this, Wilhelmina got in line behind Penny and hugged her stomach as she felt a strange flutter. "What's wrong? Are you feeling okay?" asked Penny. "I'm good" replied Wilhelmina. "Maybe you'd better tell Miss Harris. You look strange" Penny said with a look of concern. "No!" whispered Wilhelmina. "I can't miss the concert; Mom says I have butterflies". A confused Penny only stared at Wilhelmina.

Mr. Speed greeted the students and teachers at the door of the large music room. Wilhelmina noticed the classical music playing as they entered and wondered if it was Mozart. She said "good morning and thanks for the music". Mr. Speed chuckled. "You're welcome Wilhelmina". "I know you're as excited as I am and looking forward to our visiting Symphony Hall today. It promises to be an enjoyable time for all", he announced boldly for all to hear. Wilhelmina looked around the room at the faces of her classmates. Some of them smiled, some had frowns, and some had no expressions at all. She didn't know what to think. The teachers nodded their heads with interest, but didn't seem to share Mr. Speed's enthusiasm. Wilhelmina herself was still quite happy.

Wilhelmina and Penny sat together on the first bus. Once the other buses were loaded, they were on their way to the great Symphony Hall. Penny saw Wilhelmina holding her stomach and reminded her that Miss Harris was sitting only three seats away. "I can't say anything, and you know why" Wilhelmina told her friend. Still feeling the strange flutter, she whispered in Penny's ear; "This is our secret; this day has to be perfect". As the bus rolled on, Wilhelmina noticed that her classmates were in joyful spirits. The teachers tried to quiet the noisy bunch, but soon gave up. The bus's engine was rather noisy, too, and added to the chaos, excitement, and the butterfly flutter.

Everyone felt the bus make a wide turn. They had to hold on to their seats. Soon the bus began to move slower. As Wilhelmina turned to see what was happening, she shook her friend and shouted "There it is; Symphony Hall!" Both girls looked in awe at the gigantic glass building that seemed to reach around five city blocks. They noticed students from other schools arriving and getting off their buses. Wilhelmina even saw one of her friends from dance class. Everyone watched and waited until their drivers were signaled to pull up and let the teachers and students leave the buses.

Teachers and ushers directed students to form double lines, and Wilhelmina and Penny held hands and smiled. The lobby was bright from the sunlight streaming through sparkling glass. Large chandeliers hung from the ceiling, and made everyone look up, even if they didn't want to. There was still a big grin on Wilhelmina's face as she joined the sea of concertgoers being led through doors, up spiraling staircases, and onto elevators. As the ushers led Wilhelmina's group up a wide staircase, sounds of the various musical instruments could be heard.

Wilhelmina recognized violins, trumpets and cellos. "They're warming up" she told Penny. The girls' eyes were as big as saucers. They reached their seats and looked towards the stage. The stage lights and the yards of red velvet curtains seemed to welcome the audience, and soon only the instruments and excited whispers could be heard. Wilhelmina took a deep breath and decided to try to relax. She smiled at her best friend. "I'll ignore these butterflies as long as I can, Penny. Please keep our secret from Miss Harris." As they looked around the beautiful auditorium, they saw boys and girls smiling. Wilhelmina wondered if they, too, were anxious for the concert to begin.

Suddenly, the lights began blinking, the instruments quieted, and the audience hushed. A brilliant spotlight shone on the middle of the rich velvet curtains, and to Wilhelmina's delight, the Maestro, looking very distinguished in black tuxedo and tails, stepped onto the stage. He bowed, smiled, and cleared his throat. "Ahem", he began. "Welcome to Symphony Hall". Thunderous applause came from the audience and from Wilhelmina's butterflies. "Oh!" she said, bending over. She caught a glimpse of Miss Harris, who was caught up in the moment. "No worries yet", Wilhelmina thought.

As the curtains separated, everyone gasped at the sight of the musicians and beautiful instruments on stage. Each musician was dressed in formal attire; the men, looking a lot like the maestro, and the ladies in long, flowing gowns. They smiled as the maestro turned to them and stepped on the podium. Wilhelmina waited with wide-eyed anticipation, realizing that the concert was about to begin. The maestro held both hands up, and brought them down quickly and smooth.

At the start of Sousa's Stars and Stripes Forever, Wilhelmina recognized it. "I have that piece at home!" she yelled. The audience around her went "shush", but she didn't hear them. She was only aware of the beautiful notes coming from the instruments.

She felt the crashing of cymbals and the rich tones of the strings. Wilhelmina saw the musicians playing the timpani and other percussion instruments standing and moving around a lot. The program continued with Symphony #19 in D major, and Canon in D. As The Blue Danube Waltz played, Wilhelmina admired the lady playing the harp, and imagined dancers gliding across the front of the stage. "Exceptional!" she said to herself. Wilhelmina couldn't stop smiling. She squeezed Penny's hand, as a mesmerized audience exploded with applause at the end of each musical selection.

After a while, the maestro turned to the grateful audience and announced that the next number would be their last. "It is a surprise for this wonderful audience", he smiled.

There was silence as everyone waited, wondering what the surprise would be. Then, facing the orchestra once again, the maestro brought down the baton softly. The musicians began playing Mozart's Twinkle, Twinkle Little Star. "I know that!" beamed Penny. The audience began singing along with the orchestra. On the final note, the young concert goers clapped and shouted "APPLAUSE! APPLAUSE! BRAVO! BRAVO!" throughout the hall.

The gallery of smiles assured Wilhelmina that she might not be so misunderstood by some of her classmates after today. "This is the best day ever!" she yelled to Penny. Penny beamed with joy, and noticed that Wilhelmina wasn't holding her stomach anymore. "How do you feel?" Penny asked. Wilhelmina raised her eyebrows, held her stomach, and took a deep breath. "That's strange. I don't feel them anymore. Maybe I'm not sick; just excited about being here. Is that what Mom meant?" Then, as if announcing to the world, the two friends waved their hands in the air, proclaiming this a perfect day.

Before leaving their row, Wilhelmina pulled Penny back and turned to get another look at the stage. She could see the musicians' feet moving through the opening at the bottom of the flowing red velvet curtains, and wished she could relive this perfect day.

While a splendid recording of Sousa's Washington Post March helped the audience step quickly towards the exits, Wilhelmina's feet marched and her mind raced. She had a feeling that this would not be her last visit to Symphony Hall. "Oh!" she groaned, and happily grabbed her stomach.

SYMPHONY HALL
Young Peoples Concert
PROGRAM
Welcome Students and Teachers

Stars and Stripes Forever.................John Philip Sousa
Symphony #19 in D Major.................Michael Haydn
Canon in D...............................Johann Pachelbel
The Blue Danube Waltz.....................Johann Strauss II
Twinkle, Twinkle Little Star..............Wolfgang Amadeus Mozart
Washington Post March.....................John Philip Sousa

WILHELMINA'S NOTES

applause – Clapping hands quickly to show appreciation

brass – Wind instruments that use a cup mouthpiece to produce sound (trumpet, trombone, tuba, baritone and French horns)

classical music – Sophisticated style of music (symphonies, operas)

concert – A public musical performance

maestro – Title of respect used for the leader (conductor) of the orchestra. The conductor uses a baton to lead the orchestra, and helps the orchestra and audience understand the meaning of the music.

orchestra – A group of musicians playing string, brass, woodwind, and percussion instruments.

percussion – A family of instruments that produce hard or soft sound when struck with sticks, mallets, or hand (drums, timpani, cymbals, gong); The xylophone, marimba, vibraphone and chimes produce melodic tones when struck with a mallet or hammer.

podium – An elevated platform that holds sheets of music for an orchestra conductor.

strings – A family of instruments that uses strings to produce sound. A bow is also used to sustain the tone (violin, viola, cello, and double bass). The harp is also a member of the string family.

symphony – A detailed creation of music that produces sounds in harmony.

woodwinds – Wind instruments played using a cane reed to produce sound (clarinet, saxophone, oboe, bassoon, English horn). The flute and piccolo also belong to this family of instruments because they were once made of wood.